Mary-Denese Holmes

RHONDA THE UNICORN

AUSTIN MACAULEY PUBLISHERS™

LONDON • CAMBRIDGE • NEW YORK • SHARJAH

A CIP catalogue record for this title is available from the British Library.

ISBN 9781788238052 (Paperback)
ISBN 9781788238069 (Hardback)
ISBN 9781788238076 (E-Book)
www.austinmacauley.com

First Published (2018)
Austin Macauley Publishers™ Ltd
25 Canada Square
Canary Wharf
London
E14 5LQ

Lilly-Beatrice Holmes-Bradshaw and Pearl Holmes created the illustrations.
Text by Mary-Denese Holmes.
Lilly-Beatrice Holmes-Bradshaw is a Qualified Unicorn Expert QUE.

Dedication

Dedicated to Anni-Mai: long may she refuse other people's Lists of Requirements

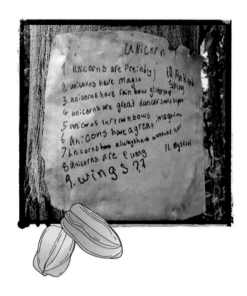

Unicorn
1. Unicorns are friendly
2. unicorns have magic
3. unicorns have rainbow glittery
4. unicorns are great dancers
5 unicorns fart rainbows
6 Unicorns have a great imagination
7 Unicorns always have awesome hair
8 Unicorns are funny
9. wings??
10. Pink
11. Mystical

Rhonda the Unicorn was fed up. She had been munching away in the nearby forest, dreaming her small unicorn dreams, when she came across a leaflet blown by the wind and now wrapped around her favourite Carambola tree.

Rhonda looked at the leaflet entitled *List of Unicorn Requirements*.

She felt pretty fed up with people needing her to be pink, perky and glittery. She quite liked the soft brownish-grey colour of her skin, and the way it looked almost pinkish at sunset, even if it was only for a short time each day. She also loved how it was goldfish red at every sunrise; surely that was beautiful enough? As for the need to be glittery, well I ask you, would you like to be glittery all the time?

Rhonda was pretty sure that being glittery would make her skin itch and twitch. Rhonda checked with her mum, who said that her soft, dusty-pink, reddish-gold colour was just right. In fact, her mum said that Rhonda had the perfect colour for a unicorn.

According to the very long *List of Unicorn Requirements*, Rhonda was supposed to be mythical and shiny. She was supposed to make people feel good. She was also supposed to be magic and could make people's wishes come true.

Rhonda felt this load of expectations was way too heavy for any young unicorn to carry. Her shoulders drooped a bit as she wondered where these ideas of being shiny and mythical had come from, and who had decided that they fit into unicorn territory?

Who had made the *List of Unicorn Requirements*, and why would they load her up with it?

Rhonda the Unicorn decided she was annoyed with people. Especially young people who expected her to fart rainbows! Where had that id-i-ot-ic idea come from? Then they wanted her to make rainbow-coloured, glittery poop. Really???

Rhonda thought and thought. Surely people only meant that her poop pile would become rainbow-ish when brightly coloured flowers and toadstools grew through the poop? Surely?

As for glittery, as well as being ridiculous, it would be sooooo scratchy! Whatever they meant by rainbow-glittery poop, Rhonda thought, people needed to go and find a hobby or read a book instead of needing things from her poop pile. The other unicorns thought her poop pile was just fine; it told them all sorts of interesting things. Rhonda's mum was quietly confident that Rhonda did not need the hassle of glitter in her poop.

Near where Rhonda lived was a soft, cool, deep water hole, full of small creatures and delicious plants. In the summer, Rhonda would visit this cool place during the hottest part of the day. Here, she would swim and play and share time with other unicorns and birds (and the tasty plants, of course!). Time spent there was normally a great delight for her. Today, however, Rhonda's thoughts once again went to the *List of Unicorn Requirements*. She remembered that it claimed unicorns were great singers and dancers.

Rhonda worried about this quite a bit. She asked her mother if great singing and dancing were powers unicorns had. Rhonda's mum said she could not imagine Rhonda singing or dancing; even though, she had dainty feet and toes.

Something she did know, however, was that Rhonda was a truly marvellous swimmer. Rhonda's mum has also seen that when Rhonda wanted a change from swimming, she would run nimbly through the trees: twisting and turning, as light as a feather, as fast as a leopard, and as flexible as pond grasses. In fact, mum said, Rhonda was perfect just as she was.

Now that Rhonda had read the *List of Unicorn Requirements*, her days felt heavy with all the new worries she had to carry. Rhonda knew her horn did not measure up to what a unicorn's horn was supposed to look like. Rhonda's horn was a bit stumpy, a bit crooked and a bit flattish at the end, where it was supposed to be pointy. Each morning, she would walk to the edge of the swimming pond and look at the reflection of her wonky horn in the still waters.

She asked the other unicorns and her bird friends to help her make a truly lovely horn. The unicorns, birds and other small creatures were happy to help. They found long trailing vines covered in flowers and wound these around and around Rhonda's horn.

Oh how amazing am I? thought Rhonda when she looked at her reflection in the pond.

As Rhonda walked around with her head held high and her wonderful flowery horn pointed to the sky, she felt extremely happy. She heard her heart sing with delight, and she almost danced on her dainty toes. Just then, she came to a boggy part of the forest.

Because her eyes were looking upward and were full of sunshine, she didn't see the soft ground and... whomp! In she fell, and her splendid horn was now covered in mud and snails and worms and bugs. *Well,* thought Rhonda as she crawled out of the smelly mud, *that didn't work for long.*

She shook off the muddy vines, and grumpily decided she didn't care what her horn looked like. It worked just fine.

Rhonda and her mum agreed that her horn was more than good enough. In fact, it was just right for a unicorn of her age.

Rhonda thought she had a great imagination. So yes, she agreed with that idea of unicorns and felt at last she could tick off at least one thing on the *List of Unicorn Requirements*.

The need to have 'totally awesome hair' was a bit trickier. She knew she had the loveliest shell-like ears —and she could move them independently—so she was extremely proud of them. She also had the loveliest eyelashes in the world. They were long and dark, and her mum said they were indeed perfect.

But, 'totally awesome hair?'

Weeeeellllll... Rhonda thought she would need some help with that one.

Again, she asked her friends, and they went rushing off to the far ends of the forest and came back with all sorts of treasures. They piled the treasures on Rhonda's head and neck, and then stood back and let out a collective sigh: "Ohhhhh, that is so beautiful! That is totally awesome, Rhonda," they said, gazing in awe at her 'hair'.

Rhonda felt truly marvellous. Her smile was luminous as she took a few quick steps. She did a twirl, made a deep curtsy, and gracefully immersed herself in the nearby pool.

As she sank in the pool, the water slowly reached her 'totally awesome hair', and the amazing creation started to slide off into the water ... Plop. Plop. Plop.

In less than two minutes, her 'totally awesome hair' was floating, bobbing and sinking into the water. All that was left on Rhonda's head was a jewel-like plum, gracefully poised just behind her shell-like ear. Ever so quietly, it too then slid past her ear and into the pool with barely a plop or a ripple.

Rhonda's friends stared, a hush settling over them. They sighed, shook themselves, and then called to her: "Never mind, Rhonda! You are totally awesome anyway. Who cares about your hair?"

Rhonda was inclined to agree, and with a big grin, she struggled out of the forest pool and ran off laughing, with her friends flying and running and leaping beside her. Rhonda's mum watched as Rhonda threw off the last remaining treasures and went hurtling into the forest, and quietly said to herself, "Now there goes one perfect unicorn."

The next morning, Rhonda decided that she would go back one last time to look at the *List of Unicorn Requirements*. The word "wings" caught her eye. Wings??? Now, she was supposed to have wings? Really, whatever for?

Her hearing was so good, she could hear a Carambola drop on the other side of the forest. She could smell if any of her friends were anywhere even slightly close by. Why didn't the *List of Unicorn Requirements* talk about those powers?

She called to her bird friends and explained her problem. Her friends were getting a little tired of how the *List of Unicorn Requirements* was taking up all Rhonda's time and imagination. But, they were loyal friends, and they set to work; each bird donating one or two of their feathers to make Rhonda a glorious pair of wings. All through the forest you could hear, "Ouch! Ouch! Ohhhh, ouch!"

Late that afternoon, her loyal bird friends staggered into the clearing with tiny bundles of feathers—and quite sore patches on their bottoms where they'd pulled out a tail feather or two. They were muttering and grumbling and generally feeling pretty fed up.

The problem of sticking all the feathers into a pair of wings required all their imaginations, and called for a lot of bird goodwill. Finally, however, they solved the problem by spitting on to the feathers and sticking one to the other.

That was slow work, and as the evening started to appear in soft pinks and purples, the birds ran out of spit. Their beaks dried up, their eyes glazed over, and they sat in a circle around their dear friend Rhonda.

They sat on their sore bottoms and called a meeting.

"Enough already, Rhonda!" they said. "We have done our best to help you meet the *List of Unicorn Requirements*, but we can give no more. We are finished, Kaput!"

Rhonda sat, listening to the tiredness and frustration in her friends' voices and quietly came to a decision.

"I am giving up on the *List of Unicorn Requirements*," she announced, "It has taken up all our time and energy. We no longer have fun in the water and no longer play in the grasses and the forest. I am too tired to carry all these worries."

"The people who made the *List of Unicorn Requirements* will have to use their own imaginations. They will have to do their own hard work to make their wishes come true. It is not my job! They can grow and colour their own 'totally awesome hair'. They can figure out why and how anyone would want to be mythical, and they can use their own spit to make crazy, useless wings."

The birds sighed with relief, and a little bit of song trilled from their tired beaks. Rhonda's unicorn friends shook their heads, let out a big breath, twitched their shell-like ears and flopped down onto the grass.

Rhonda faced towards the setting sun and proudly declared, "I am Rhonda *Rhinoceros unicornis*. I know what sort of unicorn I am; and if there is a list to be made, I'll make my own."

Rhonda's mum heard her stirring declaration, saw how her friends' spirits had lifted with relief, and she thought how truly perfect her Rhonda really was.

Rhinoceros unicornis

Rhinoceros unicornis is also called the Indian Rhinoceros, the Greater One-horned Rhino or Great Indian Rhinoceros and is native to the Indian subcontinent. It is listed as vulnerable though populations in India and Nepal are now increasing due to strict protection,

Rhinoceros unicornis lives in riverine grasslands and nearby swamps and forests. Their life span is 30-45 years. Threats to its continued survival include loss of grasslands and wetland environments and human poaching for the rhino's horn is used in traditional medicines.

This site provides more in-depth information on *Rhinoceros unicornis* as well as opportunities to adopt a Rhino to support conservation of this species:
https://www.worldwildlife.org/species/greater-one-horned-rhino

Rhinos share their homes with other valuable plants and animals. When we protect greater one-horned rhinos, we also help protect these other species. These rhinos are also a symbol of national pride in the countries where they are found, which inspires environmental stewardship among local communities. These communities also benefit from the revenue generated through rhino ecotourism.
https://www.worldwildlife.org/species/greater-one-horned-rhino